THE USA

Cath Senker

Photographs by Howard Davies

CHERRYTREE BOOKS

Distributed in the United States by
Cherrytree Books
1980 Lookout Drive
North Mankato, MN 56001

Library of Congress Cataloging-in-Publication Data
Senker, Cath.
  The USA / by Cath Senker.
    p. cm. -- (Letters from around the world)
  Includes index.
  ISBN 978-1-84234-464-4 (alk. paper)
  1. United States--Juvenile literature. 2. United States--
Social life and customs--Juvenile literature. 3. Children--
United States--Social life and customs--Juvenile
literature. I. Title. II. Series.

E156.S46 2007
973--dc22

                                    2007002063

First Edition
9 8 7 6 5 4 3 2 1

First published in 2007 by
Evans Brothers Ltd
2A Portman Mansions
Chiltern Street
London W1U 6NR

Conceived and produced by

Nutshell
MEDIA

www.nutshellmedialtd.co.uk

Editor: Polly Goodman
Designer: Tim Mayer
Map artwork: Encompass Graphics Ltd

All photographs were taken by Howard Davies, apart from:
p6: J.Vogt; p23 (top): used with permission of NYSE.

Printed in China.

Acknowledgments
The photographer would like to thank Emily and her family,
Alyssa and friends, James H. Fitzgerald, Douglaston
Memorial Day Parade, Yolanda Jamiolkowski, Christina
Valenti and the staff and pupils of Deauville Gardens
School, Robin, Drew, Judy, and Jack in New Orleans, Mark
Chesson, Sally and Jane Hindle, Laurie Cohen at the East
Side Jewish Conservancy, Rabbi Romm and the Bialystoker
Synagogue, and Herb Katz at the St. John the Divine
Cathedral for all their help.

Cover: Emily (left) with her brother Robert and sister
Nicole by their swimming pool.
Title page: Emily and her friends in the school library.
This page: The skyline of Manhattan, New York City.
Contents page: Emily shows the cakes she has made.
Glossary page: Emily and her friends in front of the school
bus, arriving at school.
Index: Robert, Nicole, and Emily with their friends.

Contents

My Country

Sunday, March 4

214 Harbor View
Copiague, NY 11726
USA

Hi Ali!

My name is Emily Renée Vogt (you say "Vote") and I'm 8 years old. I live in Copiague (say "Co-payg"), a small town on Long Island, near New York City, in the USA. My sister Nicole is 12 and my brother is 11. I like playing with my princess castle, dressing up, and playing board games.

I hope I can help with your school project on the USA.

Write back soon!

From

Emily

Here's my family. I'm in the middle, with the pink top. Mom's name is Candida and Dad's is John.

The USA is the richest country in the world. Its people come from many different countries. Most people are from European families. There are also many African Americans, and Hispanics from Latin America.

The USA's place in the world.

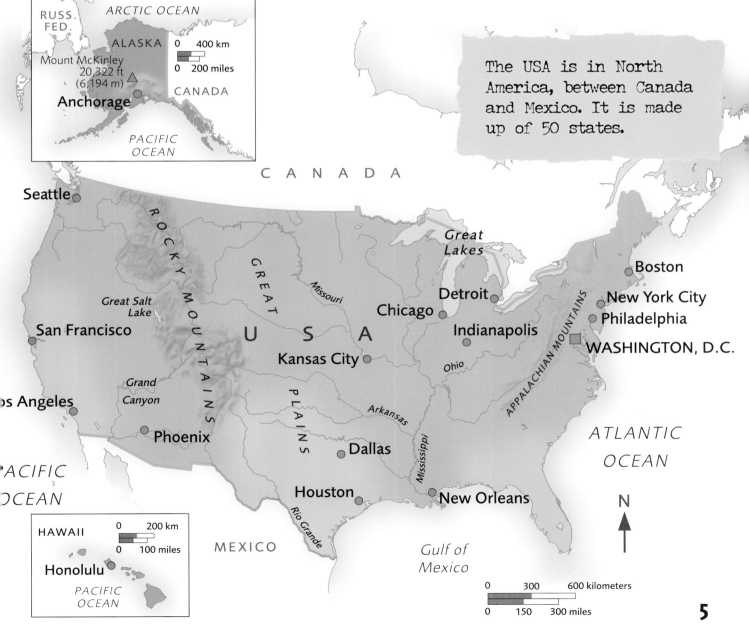

RUSS. FED.

ARCTIC OCEAN

ALASKA

Mount McKinley
20,322 ft
(6,194 m)

0   400 km
0   200 miles

CANADA

Anchorage

PACIFIC OCEAN

The USA is in North America, between Canada and Mexico. It is made up of 50 states.

CANADA

Seattle

ROCKY MOUNTAINS

GREAT

Great Lakes

Missouri

Detroit

Chicago

Boston

New York City

Philadelphia

APPALACHIAN MOUNTAINS

WASHINGTON, D.C.

Indianapolis

Great Salt Lake

San Francisco

U   S   A

Kansas City

Ohio

Los Angeles

Grand Canyon

PLAINS

Arkansas

Phoenix

Dallas

Mississippi

ATLANTIC OCEAN

PACIFIC OCEAN

Houston

New Orleans

N

Rio Grande

HAWAII

0   200 km
0   100 miles

MEXICO

Gulf of Mexico

Honolulu

PACIFIC OCEAN

0   300   600 kilometers
0   150   300 miles

5

Copiague is a small suburb by the sea. Its name comes from a Native American word meaning "sheltered harbor," because it was used as a harbor by the first people who settled there.

The suburb is on the south coast of Long Island, a large island to the east of New York City. Many people who live in Copiague, like Emily's dad, commute to the city every day for work. It takes about an hour by train to reach Manhattan, in the center of New York City.

In Copiague, most people live in large, detached houses.

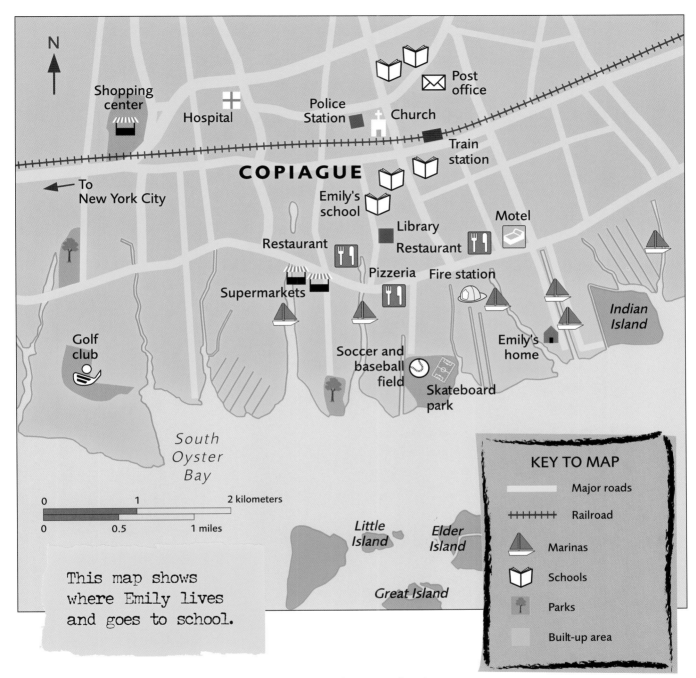

This map shows where Emily lives and goes to school.

KEY TO MAP

————	Major roads
+++++++	Railroad
⛵	Marinas
📖	Schools
🌳	Parks
	Built-up area

Many small inlets and canals run through the town, with houses and boats at their sides. Boats are also moored at marinas in some of the inlets. Just off the coast, there are several islands with beaches. In the summer, thousands of tourists visit the islands.

Landscape and Weather

The USA has many different landscapes. In the center, there is a large lowland area. To the east there are the Appalachian Mountains. The Rocky Mountains are in the west. The Great Lakes are in the northeast, and there are deserts in the southwest.

The USA suffers from tornadoes and hurricanes. A large part of New Orleans was destroyed when Hurricane Katrina hit in 2005.

Long Island has warm summers with perfect beach weather.

Much of the USA has a temperate climate, which means it is never very hot or very cold. Yet in Alaska, in the north, the climate is arctic, with temperatures dropping to −25 °F (−32 °C) in January. In the deserts of California the temperatures rise to over 120 °F (49 °C).

Long Island's Climate

January

Temperature
28 °F
(-2 °C)

Rainfall
4 in
(107 mm)

July

Temperature
72 °F
(22 °C)

Rainfall
3.2 in
(83 mm)

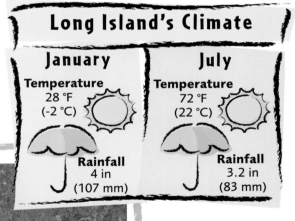

Storms can arrive quickly. This baseball game had to end suddenly when a thunderstorm took everyone by surprise.

At Home

Like about half of all Americans, Emily lives in a suburb. Only about 2 percent of the population live in the countryside. The rest mostly live in towns and cities.

Most people in American cities live in apartment buildings, like these ones in New York City.

Robert, Nicole, and Emily like riding scooters and skateboards in the street outside their house.

Emily lives in a modern house with four bedrooms, a play area, and a study. Downstairs, there is a living room, a large kitchen and a dining room. The family has a washing machine, dishwasher, TV, and DVD player.

Emily and her best friend Alyssa compete at table football in the play area. The windows have screens to keep out insects in the summer.

Outside the house there is a veranda, a front yard, and a back yard with a swimming pool. The house backs on to an inlet.

Emily and Nicole are learning how to play the piano and the clarinet. They practice in the study.

Emily's mother and her family came to the USA from the Dominican Republic when she was a baby. She and Emily's father both grew up in New York City. They moved to a larger home in Copiague when Emily was 1 year old.

Each weekend, Emily, her brother and sister help their mother by doing some cleaning and other chores.

Saturday, March 24

214 Harbor View
Copiague, NY 11726
USA

Hola! (You say "O-la." That's the Spanish word for "Hi").

Did I tell you that I speak Spanish as well as English? That's because my mom comes from the Dominican Republic, where the language is Spanish. My grandma doesn't speak much English, so I speak to her only in Spanish. She and grandpa live nearby, so we see them all the time. My cousins live all over the USA, which means we can only visit them in the vacations.

Do you speak any other languages?

Write soon!

From

Emily

Here I am in my bedroom, doing my homework. All my friends have their own computer.

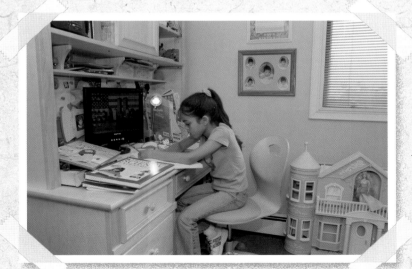

Food and Mealtimes

On schooldays, Emily and her family get up between 6:30 A.M. and 7:30 A.M. for breakfast. They have cereal, fruit, and bagels, with juice to drink. Emily usually has a cooked lunch at school, but sometimes she takes a packed lunch. For dinner, the family usually has chicken, sausages, or pasta with vegetables.

Here are Emily, Nicole, and their mother having breakfast. On weekends, they sometimes have pastries as a treat.

Emily's Uncle Ace often comes for lunch over the weekend. The family usually eats hot dogs, pizza or sweetcorn.

Like other Americans, Emily and her family enjoy hot dogs, burgers, and pizza. Sometimes they have African-American foods such as barbecued pork, black-eyed peas, and corn bread. They also like spicy Mexican food. In the summer when it is hot, Emily enjoys drinking iced tea.

On summer weekends, Emily's dad cooks sausages on the gas barbecue outside and makes hot dogs.

There is a huge choice of vegetables at the supermarket.

Emily's mother buys most of the family's food at one of the large supermarkets in Copiague. Much of the food she buys is produced in the USA. Other food comes from Canada, and beef is sometimes from South America.

Like most people in the USA, Emily and her family enjoy going out to a good Italian pizza restaurant.

Saturday, April 14

214 Harbor View
Copiague, NY 11726
USA

Hey Ali,

Here's a recipe for one of my favorite foods — cupcakes:

You need: 8 tablespoons butter, 1/2 cup sugar, 2 eggs (lightly beaten), 1 cup flour, 1 tablespoon baking powder, 1 teaspoon vanilla extract, 2 tablespoons milk.

1. Preheat the oven to 375 °F.
2. Butter a 12-hole cupcake pan or put paper cases in each hole.
3. Beat the butter and sugar in a mixing bowl until the mixture is pale and fluffy. Add the egg a little at a time, using a whisk.
4. Add the vanilla. Sift in the baking powder and half of the flour, and fold into the mixture. Add the milk and the rest of the flour. Fold until everything is well mixed.
5. Spoon the mixture into the pan. Bake for 12 minutes or until the cakes have risen and are golden on top. Allow to cool.

From

Emily

Here I am with Mom and Alyssa making cupcakes.

School Day

All American children start school in the kindergarten class at elementary school when they are 5 years old. The following year is first grade. Children move to middle school when they are 11 and high school at 14.

Like most of her friends, Emily takes the school bus to and from school. It arrives at her house at 8:15 A.M.

Emily is in the third grade at Deauville Gardens Elementary School. The school day is from 9:05 A.M. to 3:10 P.M. Lunch is from 12:20 to 1:05 P.M.

Every morning, before lessons begin, the children pledge loyalty to their country. They recite the words of the pledge together.

The school year is divided into four terms. There are short vacations in November, at Christmas, in February, and at Easter. The summer vacation is 11 weeks long.

Emily is learning how to weave. At her school, the children learn by doing things for themselves.

Emily's school has a large library, which the children go to once a week. Once a month, they visit the public library a few streets away.

Emily's main school subjects are math, English, social studies (including science), and geography. She also does music and sports. She has classes in gymnastics and plays basketball, baseball, and soccer.

Robert is watching a race on Field Day (school sports day), which is held once a year in the summer.

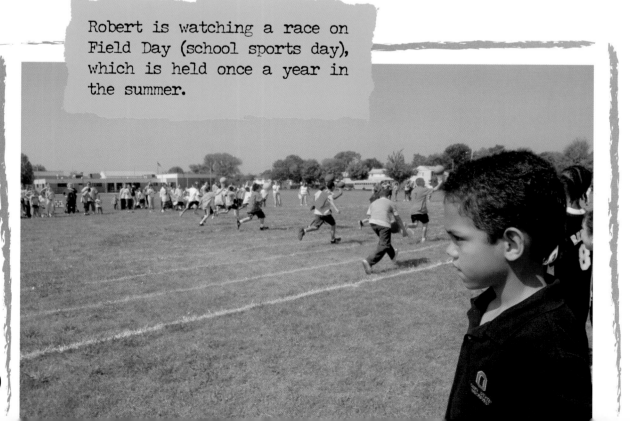

Tuesday, May 8

214 Harbor View
Copiague, NY 11726
USA

Hola Ali!

Have I told you about my school? There are 20 children in my class and over 900 in the whole school. My teacher is named Mrs. Jamiolkowski. We did a great geography project this term. We made small paper dolls called Flat Stanleys and sent them to friends and family around the USA. They took photos of them in places like Disneyland and on the beach in California, and sent them back with diaries describing what they did. They were really funny to see.

What school project are you working on at the moment?

From

Emily

↗

Here's Mrs. Jamiolkowski helping me on the computer. We have computers in every classroom. We use them for different subjects and do research on the Internet.

Off to Work

Emily's dad works for a company that makes burgers. He works in an office in Queens, part of New York City. It takes him about 45 minutes to drive there every day. The city is a center for money services, publishing, and media industries.

Many people drive to work in New York City from the suburbs. There are highways with three lanes to cope with the traffic.

This is the New York Stock Exchange, where traders buy and sell shares in companies.

The USA has many industries. Factories make cars, steel, airplanes, and electronic goods. Energy is produced from the country's own coal, natural gas, and oil reserves. Farming is important, too. Services such as banking and insurance make the most money.

This oil refinery is on the Mississippi river, in New Orleans, Louisiana. Here, oil is made into gasoline for cars.

Free Time

After school and on weekends, Emily likes going to the skateboard park, playing ball games, and going to the beach. She also enjoys swimming, trampolining in the garden, riding her scooter, and going to the movies.

At the skateboard park, Emily and her friends learn to speed up and down the ramps. Sometimes they almost fly through the air!

In the summer, Emily and Nicole often paddle a kayak out on the inlet. They wear life jackets in case they capsize.

Emily and her sister love going clothes shopping with their mother. As a special treat, the whole family sometimes goes to a big theme park nearby, with water slides and flumes. For their vacations, the family often visits Emily's aunt in Florida and then goes to Disneyland.

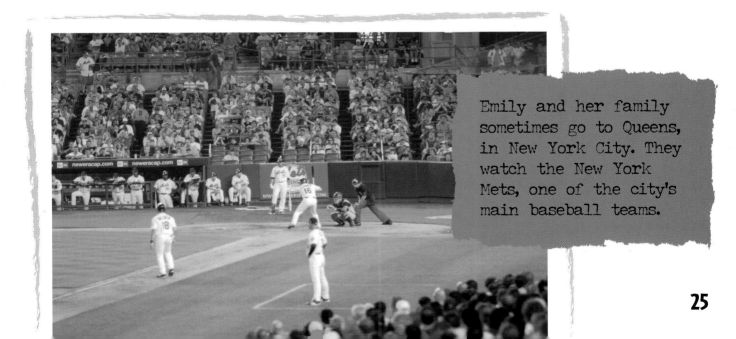

Emily and her family sometimes go to Queens, in New York City. They watch the New York Mets, one of the city's main baseball teams.

Religion and Special Days

This Christian church service is taking place in a cathedral in New York City.

Most Americans are Christians, but there are many different Christian churches. The biggest are the Protestant and Catholic churches. There are also about 6 million Jews and 6 million Muslims. There are growing numbers of Buddhists and Hindus, mostly people who have moved to the USA from other countries.

A Jewish rabbi reads in a synagogue in New York City. The city is home to a quarter of the USA's Jews, as well as a quarter of the country's Muslims.

Monday, May 28

214 Harbor View
Copiague, NY 11726
USA

Hi Ali,

It was really exciting here today because it was Memorial Day. This is a holiday all over the USA, when we remember all the American soldiers who have died in wars. There are big parades in many towns and cities. The largest parade in the country is held at Douglaston, on Long Island. It is really close to where we live. I went to watch with my friend Alyssa. We waved flags as the parade went by. It was a baking hot day and the parade was more than a mile long, so it took about four hours to pass by!

Hasta pronto! (That's Spanish for "See you soon!")

From
Emily

Here I am with my friend Alyssa, waving our flags at the Memorial Day parade.

Fact File

Capital City: Washington, D.C. The president lives and works in the White House.

Other Major Cities: New York, Los Angeles, Chicago, and Philadelphia.

Size: 3,702,318 square miles (9,631,420 km^2)

Population: 298,444,215

Languages: English is the main language of the USA. About 11 percent of the population speak Spanish as their first language.

Motto: The national motto is "In God We Trust".

Main Religions: About 78 percent of Americans are Christian. About 1 percent are Jewish and 1 percent are Muslim. About 10 percent follow other religions, while 10 percent do not follow any religion at all.

Flag: The US flag is known as the "Stars and Stripes." The 13 stripes stand for the very first colonies (European settlements) in the country. The 50 stars stand for the 50 states in the USA now. Many people feel that the flag stands for their freedoms and rights.

Main Industries: Petroleum, steel, motor vehicles, aerospace (aircraft, and equipment to go into space), telecommunications, chemicals, electronics, food processing, consumer goods (e.g. food, clothing), timber (wood), mining.

Currency: The US dollar. There are 100 cents in a US dollar.

Wildlife: In many northern areas, there are black bears, bobcats, minks, beavers, muskrats, moose, hares, red foxes, and wolves. In the eastern and southeastern forest area, there are many kinds of fish, reptiles, and birds. On the grasslands there are bison, pronghorns (like deer), and badgers. In the southwestern deserts, lizards, and snakes are found. Goats live high up in the Rocky Mountains.

Longest River: The Mississippi is about 2,350 miles (3,780 km) long.

Highest Mountain: Mount McKinley 20,322 feet (6,194 m).

Famous People: Martin Luther King, Jr. (1929–68) was a leader of the movement in the 1960s that fought for equal rights for black people. Walt Disney (1901–66) is famous for creating cartoon films and building Disneyland. Muhammad Ali (born 1942) was a world-class boxer and became a campaigner for equal rights. TV actress and talk-show hostess Oprah Winfrey (born 1954) became one of the richest women in the USA and holds great influence.

Stamps: American stamps show presidents, national parks, plants and animals, famous people, and cartoon characters.

Glossary

African American A black American who is related to people who were brought from Africa as slaves a long time ago.

arctic To do with the extremely cold region near the North Pole.

elementary school A school for children aged between 5 and 11 years old. It is also called grade school.

Hispanic A person living in the USA whose family comes from Latin America.

hurricane A violent storm with very strong winds.

inlets Narrow strips of sea water that stretch into land.

kayak A canoe with pointed ends that is covered all over apart from the seat.

kindergarten The first year at a school, which American children start when they are 5 years old.

Latin America The parts of Central and South America where Spanish or Portuguese is spoken.

pledge To make a promise.

refinery A factory where a substance is made pure, for example, oil or sugar.

shares Part of a company that people can buy. People who have shares are given some of the money that the company makes.

suburbs An area where people live that is outside the centre of a city.

tornado A violent storm with very strong winds that move in a circle.

veranda A platform built on to the side of a house on the ground floor.

Further Information

Information books:

Foster, Leila and Fox, Mary. *Continents: North America*. Heinemann First Library, 2006.

Milligan, Simon. *A River Journey: The Mississippi*. Wayland, 2005.

Symbols of America series: *The American Flag; The Fourth of July; The Liberty Bell; The Star-Spangled Banner; The Statue of Liberty; The White House*. Benchmark Books, 2004.

Fiction:

Doolittle, Bev. *The Forest Has Eyes*. Workman Publishing, 2002.

Hausman, Gerald. *The Story of Blue Elk*. Houghton Mifflin, 2001.

Memories of Cibola: Stories from New Mexico Villages. University of New Mexico Press, 2001.

Shefelman, Janice. *Young Wolf and Spirit Horse*. Random House, 1997.

St. Romain, Rose Anne. *Moon's Cloud Blanket*. Pelican Publishing, 2003.

Web sites:

Deauville Gardens Elementary School
www.copiague.k12.ny.us/minisites/dge/index.htm
The website of Emily's school.

Fact Monster
www.factmonster.com/us.html
Facts about the US government, presidents, famous people, important women, geography, and education.

Flat Stanley Project
http://flatstanley.enoreo.on.ca/
The official Flat Stanley website.

United States fauna
www.unitedstatesfauna.com
Information about animals in the USA.

The World Factbook
www.cia.gov/cia/publications/factbook/index.html
Facts and figures about the USA and other countries.

Index